For our Daughter, Sandflower: Endless waterfalls of strength,
lotus star petals & love we shower upon you, our future.

To Rudy. You are my Great Love, my Warrior Supreme & my fantasy
vision of pure love made manifest. Thank you, Master Artist. —DKD

To DK, my "Sonic, Yogini, Songstress,
Curandera," my GL, my heart! —RG

THIS IS A BORZOI BOOK PUBLISHED BY ALFRED A. KNOPF

Text copyright © 2023 by DK Dyson Jacket art and interior illustrations copyright © 2023 by Rudy Gutierrez

All rights reserved. Published in the United States by Alfred A. Knopf, an imprint of Random House Children's Books,
a division of Penguin Random House LLC, New York.

Knopf, Borzoi Books, and the colophon are registered trademarks of Penguin Random House LLC.

Visit us on the Web! rhcbooks.com Educators and librarians, for a variety of teaching tools, visit us at RHTeachersLibrarians.com

Library of Congress Cataloging-in-Publication Data
Names: Dyson, DK, author. | Gutierrez, Rudy, illustrator. Title: Window fishing / DK Dyson ; [illustrated by] Rudy Gutierrez.
Description: First edition. | New York : Alfred A. Knopf, 2023. | Audience: Grades K–1. | Summary: Amir bonds with Rudeday,
his downstairs artist neighbor, over a game they invented.
Identifiers: LCCN 2022003792 (print) | LCCN 2022003793 (ebook) | ISBN 978-0-593-42901-3 (hardcover) |
ISBN 978-0-593-42902-0 (library binding) | ISBN 978-0-593-42903-7 (ebook)
Subjects: CYAC: Games—Fiction. | Friendship—Fiction. | LCGFT: Picture books.
Classification: LCC PZ7.1.D985 Wi 2023 (print) | LCC PZ7.1.D985 (ebook) | DDC [E]—dc23

The text of this book is set in Optima LT Pro Demi Bold.
The illustrations were created as traditional mixed media acrylic paintings, inclusive of colored pencils and crayons, with digital touches.
Book design by Martha M. Rago
MANUFACTURED IN CHINA
10 9 8 7 6 5 4 3 2 1 First Edition

WINDOW FISHING

By
DK Dyson

Illustrations by
Rudy Gutierrez

Alfred A. Knopf
New York

The artist Rudeday sat at his drawing table and sighed. "Every day is the same! Painting away to make some pay."

Rudeday could draw anything! He painted pictures for magazines, newspapers, music albums, and even cereal boxes, but he complained about them all.

"I'll never be a famous artist. No one will ever know my name. My art will never bring people joy."

Sometimes Rudeday took a break from
painting and treated himself to his favorite foods—
rice and beans with plátanos, empanadas, aguacate,
ensalada, and a black-and-white cookie for dessert.
He would dance to his favorite music, but then he
would go back to being grumpy. "No time for fun
when there's work to be done."

He worked all day and most of the night, hardly ever sleeping. And when he did try to sleep, the loud noises upstairs didn't help.

BOOM!

BOOM!

BOOM!

One afternoon, Rudeday was hard at work when
he heard something outside his apartment window.

TaP!

TaP!

TaP!

Rudeday ignored it. He lived on the fourth floor,
so no one could be outside his window. Impossible!

He heard the noise again. Rudeday sucked his teeth and rolled his eyes. "I don't have time for this nonsense!"

He opened the blinds. At first, he didn't see anything. But then . . .

. . . HE SAW IT!

A piece of string on a paper clip coming from upstairs. It seemed to be saying . . .

PLAY WITH ME!

Rudeday had an idea.

Slowly, the line was reeled uP! uP! uP!

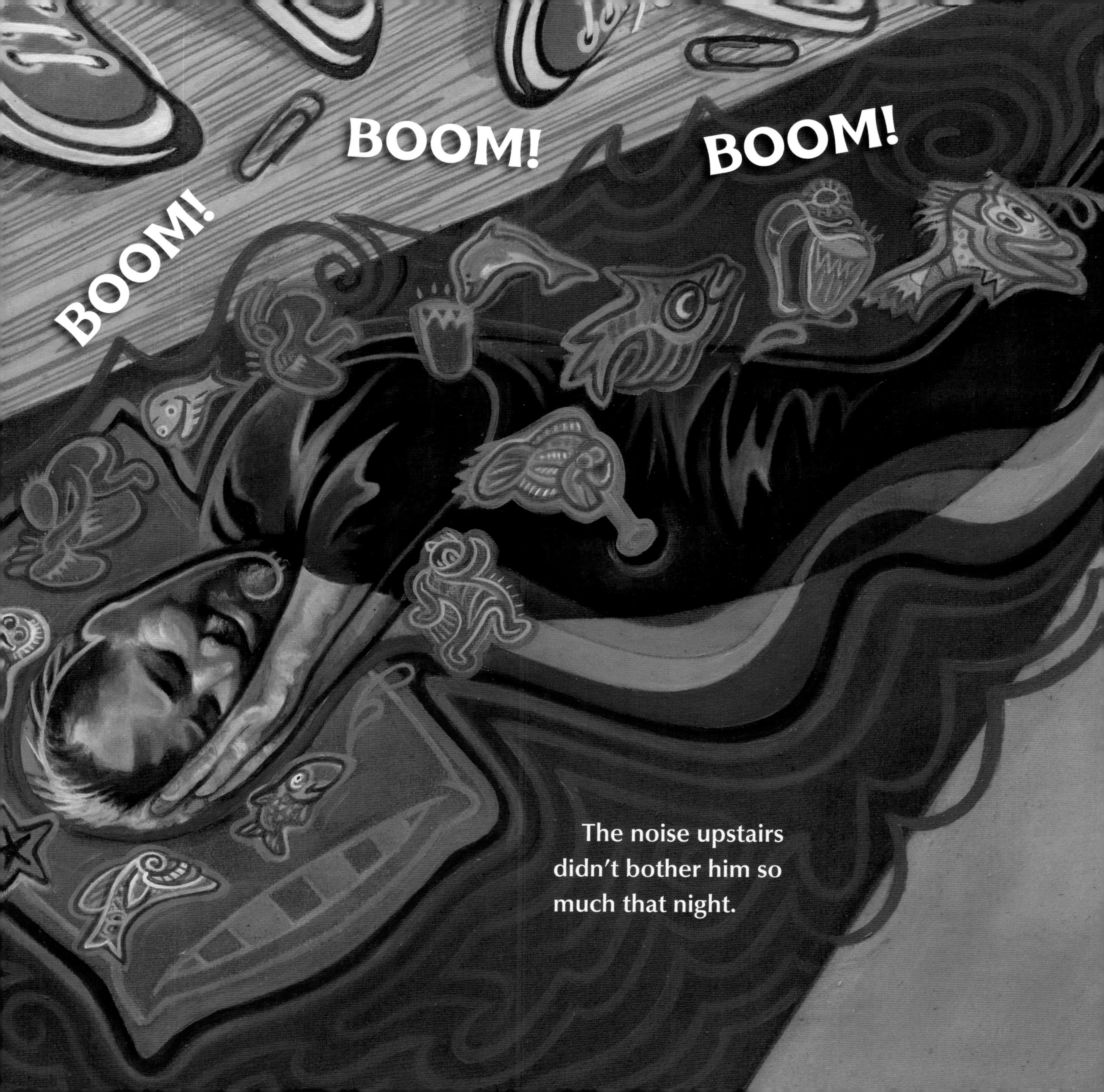

The noise upstairs didn't bother him so much that night.

The next day
it happened again.

TaP!
TaP!
TaP!

Tug!
Tug!
Tug!

Up it went!

Rudeday loved his daily window fishing.
He stopped working so much and took
breaks to dance to his favorite music—Latin,
with its big horns and fast-spinning steps.
Reggae, with its thumping bass and guitar
licks pulsing like a heartbeat. Jazz, swaying
with the harmony of saxophones and pianos.
African, with its different drumbeats
that filled him with pride
to be alive!

But then one day it stopped. No

TaP! TaP! TaP!

on the window. And no

BOOM! BOOM! BOOM!

running upstairs.

"I don't even know the name of my window-fishing friend," Rudeday sighed. He closed the blinds and went back to work.

A few weeks later, Rudeday heard a
KNOCK! KNOCK! KNOCK
on his door.

"Who is it?" he grumbled.

"Hi!" said a little boy, standing at the door with his family. "My name is Amir. I want to thank you for making me happy when I wasn't feeling well." Amir handed Rudeday a beautiful box, filled to the brim with all their drawings.

This was Rudeday's window-fishing friend!

"Well, Mr. Amir, my name is Mr. Rudeday, and I want to thank YOU for helping me learn how to have fun again!"

"I have a surprise for you," Amir said.

When he opened the blinds,
Rudeday could hardly believe
his eyes. . . .

The whole city was

WINDOW FISHING!

Rudeday was famous!
Everyone knew his name.
But best of all, his art
brought people joy.

NEWSPAPER

ARTIST AND LITTLE BOY
BRING JOY TO THE WORLD

Rudeday!

"Now," said Rudeday, passing out black-and-white cookies to his new friends, "shall we all go window fishing in our great ocean of life?"
"You bet," said Amir. "This is the reel deal!"

The next day, Rudeday heard a familiar

TaP! TaP! TaP!

on the window, and there on the line

was a message.